KAIJU SPAWN

DAVID ROBBINS AND ERIC S BROWN

SEVERED PRESS
Hobart Tasmania

KAIJU SPAWN

KAIJU SPAWN

The rain had put out the fire. The crumpled shell of the super center still smoldered, waves of dark smoke rose into an even darker sky. Most of the structural damage to the building had come from the Kaiju's foot and not the exploding propane tanks that were ignited when the great beast stepped on the store's outdoor department. No fire crews had shown up at the scene and Wally knew there wouldn't be any coming. He hunkered down under a piece of the super center's roof that remained standing and seemed safe enough to use as shelter from the rain.

The parking lot was a sea of abandoned cars, some of them crushed by the Kaiju's passing. A few of them were still stubbornly burning despite the rain. There were bodies everywhere. Some were victims of the Kaiju itself, while others were from the lesser monsters that followed in the great beast's wake. Others were trampled by fellow shoppers in the mass panic-filled attempt to flee during the Kaiju's approach. Here and there, Wally even saw an unfortunate who had died from "friendly fire" as the military had engaged the Kaiju as it was leaving the area.

A lone tank lay in the center of the parking lot, like a discarded toy. The side of its armor, where the Kaiju had kicked it aside, was caved inward. Wally wondered if any of the tank's crew was alive but he sure wasn't going out there to check and see.

As bad as the Kaiju were, the creatures that followed them were worse. No one really knew exactly what they were or how they came into being. The best guess Wally heard on the news, before the Kaiju reached Brookstown and everything hit the fan for him personally, was that Kaiju blood was some sort of mutagen. In real life, the Kaiju could be hurt much easier than the ones from the old black and white movies where it seemed the military's best weapons did little more than tick the giant monsters off. They bled when tanks and planes emptied their ordnance into them and their blood flowed freely as they continued on with their rampage. People and even animals that were exposed to the Kaiju blood changed, and not in a good way. Wally wasn't a science geek but the word infected fit what happened better than anything else. The Kaiju blood gave those who came into contact with it something akin to a never ending adrenaline rush. They were stronger, sometimes even faster, than they were before they became infected. That wouldn't have been a bad thing except it also made them nearly mindless, hungry monsters who wanted nothing but a chance to tear you apart and eat your insides. The Japanese media had dubbed those who were infected "Kaiju Spawn" before Japan had gone quiet entirely and was assumed lost.

Like most folks in the United States, Wally hadn't really been able to accept what was happening when the Kaiju rose from the oceans. Even when the military was mobilized, no one honestly believed that the Kaiju would reach the U.S. before they were stopped or that there could be so many of the Kaiju.

Most folks had simply gone on with their own lives as if they were in some sort of trance-like denial. Wally knew he had been just as guilty as everyone else. The drive up from South Carolina was a long one and when he saw the sign for the super center, he took the exit ramp to it. The radio had been blaring warnings of Kaiju headed through North Carolina but at that moment, there was no sign of them and traffic was moving along like normal. Sure, he had passed a few troop transport trucks and noticed a helicopter or two in the air but he had a deadline to keep. Leigh was waiting on him in Sylva and nothing ever happened in that small town. He'd grown up there, so he could attest to that fact with certainty. Besides, as much as he hated Claudia, he knew she was a good mom when push came to shove. She would keep Leigh safe until he got there to pick her up for the weekend.

His plan had been to stop at the super center, pick up Leigh a spur of the moment gift, and grab an energy drink. Wally hadn't realized his quest to find the latest Wonder Woman toy was going to turn into a life and death struggle for survival. Things like that didn't happen in America, much less the rural south.

He had been on his way inside when the Kaiju showed up. The great beast came lumbering down the interstate towards the super center, an unstoppable juggernaut of fury. Wally had stared at the thing in disbelief until the ex-army part of his brain took over. Then he had run like Hades to find cover in the woods that surrounded the super center. From there, he had watched it all as the Kaiju destroyed the store, slugged it out with the military units pursuing it, and moved on after they had been dealt with.

Wally stayed in the trees until long after the Kaiju and a fresh batch of Kaiju Spawn that had been infected during the battle rose up and followed after it. Only then, as the rain began to pour, did he leave the safety of the trees. His car, like many others, was crushed during the battle. It took him close to half an hour to pull and force his way inside the car enough to reach the pistol he kept in its glove box. Thankfully, the gun was undamaged and fine.

Now armed, he cautiously headed into the remains of the store to take shelter from the rain. His hands were trembling as he clutched the pistol and truly took in the destruction around him. If there was anyone else who had survived and not fled, there was no sign of them. Wally sat down his pistol and dug in his pocket for his phone. He hit the speed dial for Claudia's number but there was no answer. The call didn't even make it to her voice mail. Instead all he got was an error message saying there was trouble with the service. Wally tried twice more before he gave up and tucked the phone away again.

Staying here was a very bad idea. Though most Kaiju Spawn did tend to follow the beast that changed them into what they were, some didn't. The last thing he wanted was to come face to face with a pack of those snarling abominations that had spread out to search the area for prey.

More than anything though, he needed to get to Sylva. His little girl was waiting for him there and nothing on this Earth was going to stop him from getting to her.

****

Wally needed wheels. He picked up his pistol, a Colt M1911 that once belonged to his grandfather, and was about to go in search of a vehicle when a crushed candy machine caught his eye. Part of the ceiling had collapsed under the Kaiju's onslaught and a slab of concrete had burst the machine as if it were a bubble, scattering candy bars and bags all over.

Wally's stomach growled, reminding him that he'd skipped breakfast because he wanted to get an early start. Hurriedly scooping up half a dozen chocolate bars, he stuffed them in his pockets.

As he turned toward the shattered window through which he'd entered, Wally froze. From outside came a sharp sound, like the grating of metal on metal. He waited for it to be repeated, and when it wasn't, decided it must be more debris collapsing.

Time to get out of there, Wally told himself. The rain had tapered, enough that he could see the far end of the parking lot where several undamaged cars were parked.

Hunching low against the drizzle, Wally stepped through the opening, careful of the jagged glass. He went a couple of steps and heard a new sound; the distant *thoom-thoom-thoom* of enormously heavy footsteps.

The Kaiju. Wally peered into the drizzle but couldn't see it. He was sure it was still moving away from the shopping center, so he felt safe in continuing toward the undamaged cars. He was halfway there when he skirted a burning pickup and couldn't avoid a streaming cloud of acrid smoke that got into his nose and mouth and stung his eyes.

Swatting and coughing, Wally emerged into clear air and froze a second time.

A creature had appeared from between the rows of smashed vehicles. Stooped over, it moved with a shambling gait. Its clothes were in tatters. The same could be said of its body. Once a woman, the mutagenic properties of the Kaiju's blood had turned her into something else, something distinctly reptilian, with hideous sores that resembled scales, and a face twisted with inhuman madness.

Wally stayed perfectly still, scarcely breathing, hoping she wouldn't notice him. No such luck. Her head rose and she sniffed loudly, like a bloodhound on a scent. The next moment, she whirled and let out a hiss like that of the Kaiju itself, although not nearly as loud.

With a shriek like that of a hawk diving for the kill, the Kaiju Spawn bounded toward him, incredibly swift.

Jerking the M1911, Wally pointed the pistol and squeezed. Nothing happened. He'd forgotten to chamber a round when he took it out of the glove compartment.

In a panic, Wally sought to remedy his mistake but it was too late. The Kaiju Spawn was on him. Fingers hooked like claws raked at his face even as she threw herself bodily at his chest, seeking to bowl him over. Somehow he got his arm up to ward off her nails but the impact knocked him back and he stumbled and nearly fell.

Before Wally could regain his balance, the Kaiju Spawn sprang. Her lips were inches from his throat, her hot breath fanning his skin, when her head exploded in a shower of gore and brains.

Belatedly, Wally registered the shot that killed her. She sprawled against him, and in revulsion he shoved her off.

"That was awful close, mister. You're damn lucky I was here."

It was another woman, only this one had sane blue eyes and close-cropped red hair, and was wearing a torn uniform. She had come from the direction of the squashed tank. Her helmet was missing, and there was a nasty welt on her forehead.

"Who....?" Wally blurted.

"Corporal Loretta Martin, 252nd Armor Regiment, North Carolina Army National Guard." As she answered him, she ejected the magazine on her M16, checked it, and slapped it back in. "Do you live around here?"

"No. I'm on my way to Sylva. My daughter….." Wally didn't go into detail. He was anxious to get out of there.

"You have a car?"

Wally pointed at the pile of pulverized metal that had once been his jeep.

Just then the Kaiju let out a roar that, despite the distance, seemed to shake the very ground.

"Did you hear that thing?" Corporal Martin said in awe.

"How could I not?" Wally made for the end of the parking lot. He'd wasted too much time as it was.

"Wait," Martin said, hobbling to catch up.

Only then did Wally realize she was hurt. Blood stained her left pant leg from below her knee to her foot. "You should contact your unit and get medical help."

"Can't. The radio in the tank is in pieces, my cell

phone won't work, and the land lines are down. And I don't need a medic." Corporal Martin glanced about them. "What I do need is to get hell and gone before more of those things show up."

"You handled that last one really well."

"I don't mean the mutations," Corporal Martin said. "I mean the monsters. Those Kaiju."

"I'd like to help. Really," Wally said. "But I have to be sure my little girl is safe." That, more than anything else.

"I'll go with you then." Martin gripped his shoulder, forcing him to halt. "Look. We're the only two people left out of the hundreds who were here when the Kaiju attacked. We should stick together for our mutual protection, if for no other reason." She paused. "Besides, you might need me after a while, whether you know it or not."

Impatient to be off, Wally said, "How so?"

"Didn't you tell me that you're headed for Sylva?"

"Yeah. So?"

"Don't your ears work? Give a listen to gruesome."

Puzzled, Wally titled his head. From afar came

the thud of giant footsteps, like the beating of a bass drum amplified a thousand times. "It's loud enough to be heard for miles. Again, so what?"

"You still don't get it?" Corporal Martin said. "Which direction is Sylva from here?"

Wally had to think a second. "Northwest," he remembered.

"And which direction is the Kaiju headed?"

Wally took a half-step, his blood turning to ice in his veins. "No!" he exclaimed.

"Took you long enough," Corporal Martin said, and gave him a lopsided grin. "Now do we haul ass, or what?"

****

The corporal was right and Wally knew it. He wanted to head out on foot but Martin convinced him otherwise. If they could find a functioning car somewhere in the devastated parking lot, the time it would save them in the long run would make it well worth their while to do so.

Wally sat in the driver's seat of an intact Ford pickup. The truck was old; its paint flaking from its body, but it was the best vehicle they had found so far. He didn't really have a clue how to hotwire a car but it looked easy enough in all the movies he had seen over the years.

"You don't have any idea how what you're doing, do you?" Martin asked.

"You wanna take a shot?" Wally snapped at her in frustration.

Corporal Martin stood off to the side of the truck, her pistol held ready in a two handed grip, as her eyes scanned the area around them. She had slung her M-16 over her shoulder.

"I'd love to but someone has to stand watch," she growled back at him.

"And you don't trust me to do it?"

Martin's lips tipped upwards in a smile. "No," she shook her head, "Not really."

Returning his attention to the wires he was flicking together, Wally suddenly got lucky. The wires sparked and the truck's engine came to life.

He slammed the driver's door, tugging on his seatbelt, as he called to Martin through the rolled down window next to him. "Hop in if you're coming!"

Martin sprinted around the truck and slid into its passenger seat. "You sure you can drive this thing?"

"I guess we'll find out," Wally shrugged. He shifted the truck into reverse and backed out of the space it sat in. Flooring the gas, he slung the steering wheel hard to the left and then the right, dodging the remains of the other cars scattered about in the lot.

When they hit the interstate, it was strangely clear. There were a few wrecks, here and there, but overall they had the road to themselves.

"This was a great idea," Wally admitted. "We should make it to Sylva by nightfall."

"Let's just hope the Kaiju isn't waiting for us when we get there," Martin commented.

"Just because it was headed northwest the last time we saw it, doesn't mean that was where the thing is going. A lot could happen along the way that would cause the monster to change its course."

"Are you always like this?" Martin asked.

"Like what?" Wally answered, frowning, but keeping his eyes glued to the road ahead of them.

"Optimistic. It's kind of annoying."

"Not at all," Wally laughed. "I'm usually quite the downer."

"But the end of the world has changed you,

huh?"

"My daughter is out there," Wally said. "I have to be optimistic."

He paused before asking, "You have any kids?"

Martin scowled at him. "I'm twenty two and career military. Do you think I have any kids?"

Wally shrugged. "Stranger things have happened."

"Yeah, like giant monsters rising up out of the oceans and people getting turned into zombies by their blood," Martin rolled up her window. "That kind of strange?"

"No need to be sarcastic," Wally pointed out.

"No," Martin said, answering his question. "I don't have any kids. I don't even really have any family to speak of."

"Then there's no way you could understand what I'm going through right now, okay? So how about cutting me some slack? It was your idea for the two of us to stick together anyhow."

"Point," Martin conceded.

They drove on for a while in silence before Martin nudged him. "Look at that," she warned him.

Up ahead, in the distance, an overturned minivan

rested on its side in the middle of the road. Around it, a pack of Kaiju Spawn were gathered. The creatures weren't trying to get into the van; they looked as if they were simply waiting on another vehicle to pass through. One of the Spawn, more transformed than the others, sat atop the van's skyward facing side. A long, sharp pointed tongue flicked out of its mouth as if the thing was tasting the air. Its yellow eyes glowed even in the light of the late afternoon sun above.

"Oh crap!" Wally shouted.

The old Ford blew past the creatures doing sixty. Several of the things leaped at the truck, but only one managed to sink its claws into the truck's side. It hauled itself up and over the side of the pickup's bed, to land on its feet behind the driver compartment with a loud thud.

The other Kaiju Spawn were chasing after the pickup as the one in its bed rammed a fist through the rear window. Shards of broken glass exploded into the truck's cabin. Wally shrieked in pain as some of them peppered the back of his neck, slicing into it like tiny razors.

"Kill it! Kill it!" Wally was screaming, as Martin

was already shifting around in her seat to bring her pistol to bear on the Kaiju Spawn. The thing laid its head back in a mighty roar that dwarfed the noise of the pickup's straining engine.

Wally flinched, gritting his teeth, as Martin's pistol cracked twice beside his ear. The road in front of the speeding truck was mostly clear so he risked a glance into the rearview mirror.

Martin's first shot caught the Kaiju Spawn in its left shoulder. Orange blood splattered into the air as the bullet tore clear through it. The Spawn's roar became an angry hiss as it threw itself forward towards the truck's cabin again. Martin's second shot met it, impacting with the side of the thing's face. Teeth flew from its open mouth as the bullet broke apart its jaw bone and ripped a large exit hole, at an angle, just under its left eye. The Spawn stumbled, toppling from the truck's bed, to go rolling and bouncing along the road in the truck's wake.

Wally could feel the warmness of his own blood flowing over his skin, running down, to seep into the cloth of his shirt. His knuckles were white from his grip on the steering wheel as he kept the gas pedal floored.

Not daring to risk another look into the rearview mirror, Wally kept his focus on the road. After a few minutes ticked by, he finally caved in and asked, "Did we lose them?"

"Yeah," Martin told him. "The Kaiju Spawn are fast but not fast enough to keep up with the rate you're driving."

Wally stole a glance at the speedometer. He was pushing eighty and still accelerating. He didn't see the curve coming up until it was too late. The truck jumped the side of the road and plowed into an embankment. The last thing he heard was the sound of the hood of the truck folding up in front of him.

****

Wally came awake with a start as if someone had plunged a needle full of adrenaline into his heart. His head jerked from side to side as he took in his surroundings. His seatbelt had saved his life. Of that, he was sure. Martin was sprawled out in the passenger seat next time him.

The corporal was unconscious, her forehead smeared with blood from where it had struck the forward windshield. The windshield was cracked and dented outward but the thick glass had held together. He couldn't tell if she was still alive or not.

Panic filled him as he remembered the Kaiju Spawn that had been chasing them. He clawed at his seatbelt's release until it popped loose. His Colt M1911 had been thrown into the floorboard at his feet from the impact of the crash. Grabbing it up, he flung his door open and staggered out of the truck. It didn't take a mechanic to see that the vehicle was totaled.

The road stretching to the horizon was clear and there was no sign of the Kaiju Spawn moving about in the woods either. Pain rippled through his chest. Wally lifted up his shirt to see the huge bruise that had formed there from where he had been flung into the steering wheel despite his seatbelt. Again, he counted his blessings. Things could have been a lot worse.

He heard Martin groan as she stirred inside the truck. Her door came open and she flopped out onto the grass of the embankment. Wally rushed to kneel beside her.

"You okay?" He asked.

Martin stared up at him with eyes racked by agony. She tried to get up and failed, twisting her body sideways to vomit up the contents of her guts.

"Not doing so good," she gasped.

"We can't stay here," Wally stated the obvious. They were all right for the moment but that could change at any moment.

"I know," Martin said, wiping her mouth with her sleeve. "You're impatient to see your daughter."

"It's not that so much," Wally said, even though, deep down, that was all that mattered to him. "Can you walk? If I help you?"

"Let's find out," Martin said, gamely smiling despite her torment.

His arm wrapped firmly, Wally started off. It surprised him, how light she was. Then again, now that he gave her a closer look, she was on the skinny side. She couldn't weigh more than a hundred and ten pounds, if that. Her loose-fitting uniform had given the impression she was heftier.

"We need another vehicle," Martin mentioned.

Wally grunted. They were going around the curve, and up ahead was a remarkable sight.

The tail end of a tractor-trailer jutted at the sky. It looked for all the world as if the cab and the front half of the trailer had been smashed grill-first into the ground and been partially buried.

As they drew nearer, Wally saw that wasn't the case. The roadway seemed to end at a jagged edge. From below and beyond came strange slithery sounds unlike any he'd ever heard.

"What in the world?" Corporal Martin blurted.

"Beats me," Wally said.

"Was there an earthquake?" Martin said.

That wasn't it at all, as they soon discovered. The big rig had plunged into a giant print left when the Kaiju, which must have weighed upward of fifty tons, had caused the roadway to buckle. Like a sink hole, the ground had given way to a depth of forty or fifty feet. The trucker had slammed on his brakes---skid marks clearly showed where the rig had swerved like crazy---but been unable to stop and gone over the edge.

"Dear God," Martin said.

"We have to go around," Wally said, and turned to do so. But no sooner did he take a couple of steps than the strange sounds issued out of the hole again.

Craning his neck, Wally peered down, and wished he hadn't. His skin crawled in sheer horror.

In the dark shadow at the bottom of the footprint, something moved. Something huge, and partially pinned by the tractor trailer. Black hide with sheen like patent leather, rippled obscenely as the thing struggled to free itself. No arms or legs were visible. No head, either.

Wally couldn't make sense of it. The part he could see resembled nothing so much as a thick tube, about six-feet around. Then the near end rose into the air and opened to reveal a maw rimmed by inward-curving saber-like teeth. There were no eyes, no nose, nothing but the mouth. It hissed, and he stopped cold in consternation.

"What in heaven's name......?" Corporal Martin said in amazement.

A tiny part of Wally's mind screamed at him to shoot but he stood mesmerized as the creature reared even higher and poised as if about to strike.

"Let go of me," Martin said, fumbling to unlimber her M16.

Wally complied. He wanted both hands free to steady the Colt anyway. As he adopted a combat stand and took deliberate aim, he remembered his last sight of the gigantic Kaiju as it stomped away from the shopping center. Remembered several long black ridges low down on the Kaiju's enormous legs. He hadn't given them any thought at the time. He was too astounded by the monster itself. But now that he did, he realized the black things hadn't been part of the Kaiju. They were whatever this thing was.

"Shoot!" Martin bawled.

Wally fired twice, the Colt bucking and booming. He saw the slugs strike. He even heard the fleshy thwack-thwack of the impacts. But the shots appeared to have no more effect than if he had used a pea-shooter.

The creature struck.

In pure reflex, Wally dived to one side. He smelled a vile odor and looked up to find the aberration's mouth spread wide above him. He tensed, thinking his time had come.

Corporal Martin cut loose. She staggered in close, and with the M16 on full auto, stitched the thing from right to left and back again.

Recoiling, the thing collapsed in on itself, like

one of those toys made of springs that Leigh played with a lot when she was younger.

"Run!" Martin urged, and tried to take her own advice but she only managed a few steps when she stumbled and would have fallen if Wally hadn't gotten to her and wrapped his arm around her waist. Blood was trickling from her mouth and she gasped as he hustled her away from the hole.

Afraid the thing would rear up again, Wally kept his head turned until they'd gone far enough that he felt safe. Slowing, he remarked, "That's twice you've saved my life."

"Who's counting?" Martin said, and succumbed to a fit of coughing that went on and on.

"That's doesn't sound good," Wally said when she subsided.

"Leech," Martin said.

"Say what?" Wally replied, not sure if he had heard correctly.

"That thing back there. I've had one stuck on me before, the time our unit was doing maneuvers in a swamp. It got on my leg and was sucking my blood. Except for all those teeth, or whatever they were, that's what that thing was. It must have been on the

Kaiju and fell off."

"Just our luck," Wally said. He scanned the road ahead for movement but there were only smashed and broken vehicles and more than a few bodies.

"Listen," Martin said.

Wally had already heard the distant thoom of the Kaiju's ponderous tread. "It's not moving very fast. If we can find another car or truck, we can circle ahead and reach my daughter in plenty of time."

"I love an optimist," Martin said, only partially sarcastically.

In a quarter of a mile they came on another pickup. It had gone down a short embankment into a ditch, and Wally would have passed it by, thinking it must be too damaged to be of any use, when he spied part of a bare leg and a shoe sticking out the open driver's door---and the leg moved. "Someone is alive in there."

Martin had recovered enough from the accident that she was able to walk with only the slightest assistance. Quite obviously, though, she was still in a lot of pain. Wiping at her mouth with her sleeve, she said, "Let's check it out."

The leg was scrawny and laced with varicose

veins. The shoe had been in vogue decades ago. The same with the dress the driver had on. So it was no surprise to Wally to discover that the woman must be in her sixties, if not older. He released Martin, who leaned against the pickup, while he slid an arm under the old woman and eased her into an upright position. She gave a start and her eyes snapped open, twin mirrors of pure fear.

"What? Who? That thing! That horrible monstrosity!"

"You're all right, lady," Wally said. "Looks as if you hit your forehead on the steering wheel."

"I did?" the old woman said, and gingerly touched a welt on her brow. "Oh. Now I remember. That monster came up behind me. I was so stunned, I let up on the gas. And when I saw it might step on me, I ran off the highway to avoid it."

"You did good," Wally said. The pickup appeared to be intact. Best of all, the keys were in the ignition. "This is Corporal Martin," he said by way of introduction. Then, "And we'd like to borrow your truck, if you don't mind."

"I beg your pardon?"

"He has a little girl he needs to save,"

Martin said. "And he has to get there fast." She frowned. "But he'll be doing it without me."

"I will?" Wally said.

"I'm hurting," Corporal Martin said. "I think I'm busted up inside. It's best if you and this lady go on without me. I'd only slow you down."

"Hold on," the older woman said, and pointed at a hill a few hundred feet away. "I live just on the other side, there. We can walk it, if you're up to it, dearie, and I can tend you. That way your friend can borrow my truck and go on, quick."

"You'd let me?" Wally said. He wasn't sure he had it in him to lend his own car to a complete stranger.

"Why not? You have a little girl, she said," the old woman replied. "Help me out and you can back up and be on your way."

Wally didn't argue. Leigh came before all else. It was only as he was speeding off that he glanced in the rear-view mirror and saw Corporal Martin and the old woman smile and wave that he realized he hadn't gotten her name. No matter. Once Leigh was safe, he'd make it a point to return the pickup.

Provided he lived that long.

****

Getting the pickup out of the ditch hadn't been an issue. The truck was four wheel drive and a pretty powerful vehicle. The damage done to it when the old lady had driven it off the road appeared to be mostly cosmetic. Wally was glad the old lady had just given it to him on faith. If she hadn't, Wally didn't want to think about what he might have done to get it. The old world's way of doing things died more and more each day. Civilization, if not already dead, was hanging on by a thread. One could make an argument that in parts of the country, the United States was a good bit of the way back to the law of the gun even before the Kaiju rose up from their slumber. Now . . . It was like the Old West all over again. If you had the power, you took what you needed to keep you and those you loved alive. At least that was the closest thing he could equate the current state of America with.

Wally hoped the Corporal and the old lady would survive until he found Leigh and returned but in truth, he didn't really have the time to think about them anymore. Either they would or they wouldn't and there was nothing he could do about it.

The road ahead of him wasn't nearly as congested with wrecked and abandoned cars as the interstate had been. Still, he kept his attention glued to the road. Wally had learned the hard way just how fast things could change. His foot was heavy on the gas pedal as he rounded a turn a little too fast and had to fight with the steering wheel to keep the pickup from going out of control. Cursing himself for being careless, Wally let out an audible sigh of relief as the road straightened out again. Exhaustion and stress were catching up with him now that there was no immediate danger in sight. He hadn't seen any Kaiju Spawn since the encounter he and the good corporal had with the Kaiju leech. That thing had creeped the heck out of him. There sure hadn't been any reports of things like it existing before all the radio stations and such had gone off the air.

His M1911 sat on the seat next to him within easy reach. He knew there were only a few rounds left in its magazine. Having the Corporal's M-16 to go with it would have made him feel a lot better but he hadn't dared ask Martin for it. As beat up as she was, her and the old lady were going to need everything they had just to hold on if a pack of Kaiju Spawn sniffed out wherever the two of them ended up digging in. He could imagine the monsters finding the two of them at the old lady's house. Kaiju Spawn claws rending wood as they tore through the front door and dozens of the creatures came pouring inside. Wally shuddered and stole a glance up at the sky. He had lost track of how long he had been driving but he knew he had put a good distance between himself and where he had left the two women. If he got into trouble again, the corporal wouldn't be around to save him this time.

Night was falling. The sun was sinking from the sky and the shadows were growing deeper in the woods lining the road. Soon, Wally would either need to turn on the pickup's headlights or abandon the truck to continue towards Sylva on foot. If he gave up the truck, it would slow him down greatly. Wally wasn't sure he was willing to risk turning on the lights. They would draw any Kaiju Spawn in the area to him like flies to a rotting corpse. Driving without them was just as great a risk. Sure, the road was clearer here but that wasn't the same as entirely clear. His night vision wasn't very good, never had been. The last thing he needed was to plow into one of the scattered cars he was still passing from time to time or misjudge a turn in the darkness.

Wally slowed the pickup as he noticed there was some kind of roadblock up ahead. It looked military in nature. There were two large lights set up on either side of a large transport truck that had been turned sideways in the roadway. He could see what appeared to be a machine gun emplacement in the truck's bed. The military setting up a roadblock here, on the outskirts of Sylva, made sense. What didn't make sense was the lack of personnel at it. There were no soldiers to order him to stop and no gunner behind the machine gun. Wally stopped anyhow. Driving around the roadblock wasn't an option due to the woods surrounding the road. The pickup he drove would never fit through the small space left open between the ends of the truck and the trees. Wally came to a stop and killed the pickup's engine. He sat staring at the roadblock, wondering what to do. No matter how much he didn't want to, he was going to have to get out of the pickup.

Reaching over, Wally grabbed his pistol, took a breath to steel himself and swung open the pickup's door. With his M1911 held ready, he cautiously advanced on the roadblock. There was still no sign of anyone nearby. As he continued to creep forward, the smell hit him. It nearly made him gag. He raised his free hand to cover his mouth and nose. The place stunk of offal, blood, and decay. There was something else in the smell too, something that reminded him of a fish market or a stagnant body of water.

Wally froze as he saw movement in the bed of the parked transport. A blood smeared, reptilian face rose up over the side of the truck's bed, its yellow eyes locking onto him. Wally felt his bladder let loose as a warm trickle of urine soaked the center of his pants between his legs and ran down the lengths of his legs. He jerked up his pistol, taking aim at the snarling face of the monster. It jumped erect in the bed of the truck as Wally squeezed the M1911's trigger. The shot sparked off the edge of the truck bed as the Kaiju Spawn gave an inhuman roar of anger and leaped towards him. The creature landed only a few feet from where he stood.   Wally barely had time to readjust his aim and get off a second shot before it came charging into him. The round from the M1911 blew a chunk of meat from the once human thing's shoulder. It was howling in pain as it struck him. Wally felt the Kaiju Spawn's claws rake across his chest in the instant before they hit the asphalt of the road with the creature on top of him. Only dumb luck saved his life. The barrel of the M1911 was angled into the Kaiju Spawn's temple when the impact jarred him just enough to cause him to involuntarily squeeze its trigger again. The shot ripped through the side of the Kaiju Spawn's skull and exited its other side in an explosion of flying brain matter and bone fragments.   The Kaiju Spawn's heavy form went limp over him.   With a grunt, he heaved its corpse upwards enough to roll it off of him.

If there had been more of the creatures, he would have been dead. Apparently, it had been alone though because in the wake of the gunshot, the falling night was quiet once more except for the panting noise of his panicked breaths.

Wally lay there in a puddle of his own urine, covered in splattered Kaiju Spawn blood, for a solid two minutes before he found the strength and nerve to move again. He realized with a start that he had no idea if the Kaiju Spawn blood was as infectious as that of a real Kaiju's or not. His heart pounding inside him, he raced the rest of the way to the transport truck, desperately searching for something to wash himself off with. He pulled himself up to peer into the bed of the truck and wished he hadn't. What he saw put him onto his knees, throwing up what was left of the contents of his stomach. Inside the truck bed were piles of detached human limbs and the shredded, gnawed upon, torsos of the soldiers who must have been assigned to hold the road.

When his body finally stopped shaking from the dry heaves tearing through it, Wally wriggled out of his shirt, turning it inside out and used it as best he could to wipe away the Kaiju Spawn blood on his skin. None of the blood had gotten into his eyes or mouth thanks to the angle of the shot that had sent the Kaiju Spawn to Hell where it belonged. At least not so far as he could tell. He still felt like a human being. That was a good sign. Wally figured if he made it through the next few minutes, he was okay. He didn't know a lot about the transformation into Kaiju Spawn but he did know it was supposed to happen very quickly.

He sat down near the transport truck and held the barrel of his M1911 pressed against the underside of his chin as he watched the seconds tick slowly by on his watch. It was the longest ten minutes of his life at the end of which he decided he must really be okay. The infection he feared hadn't been passed onto him by the wound from the Kaiju Spawn.

Wally got to his feet and conducted a quick search of the truck and the two jeeps that he discovered parked behind it. He found several bottles of water and used all but one of them, to further clean himself up and wash out the wound where the Kaiju Spawn's claws had slashed open his skin. The final one he chugged down in a series of rapid gulps.

He doubted very much that a single Kaiju Spawn could have killed all the soldiers here. Wally was NOT going to look into the bed of the truck again but his memory of the horror he had seen, told him there had to have been around half a dozen men at this roadblock based on the number of arms and legs he had seen stacked in piles. That meant that were likely more of the creatures close by but not so close as to have heard the shots he had fired or they would have been on him already. Even so, the sooner he got out of here, the better.

Wally had found a P-90 and several magazines for it in one of the jeeps. He wasn't a gun nut by any means but he had watched enough SF TV shows to recognize the P-90 for what it was. He had always thought it was one of the coolest looking guns in the world. Wally practiced ejecting and reloading its magazine until he was sure he had gotten a feel for it. He also found a small satchel of grenades in the second jeep. He tucked his pistol under his belt, shrugged the satchel of grenades onto his shoulder, and double checked to make sure the P-90 had a full mag, before setting out again towards Sylva on foot. He knew he could have moved the transport truck so that he could get his pickup through, but didn't want to chance drawing the attention of more Kaiju Spawn from the sound of the motors.

Night had fallen completely by the time he left the roadblock behind. He kept a steady pace and stuck to the center of the road as he walked. The dark clouds of the earlier rain had parted and the moon had come out. It gave him just enough light to see by. He passed a sign that read "Welcome to Sylva" and was comforted by it. Wally guessed he had about two hours or so to go before he reached the house he had grown up in and Claudia had taken from him in their divorce.

****

Sylva was a cemetery; the houses arrayed like tombstones, their windows so many dark eyes. It gave Wally a creepy feeling to think that real eyes might be peering out at him. Inhuman eyes, belonging to creatures that would rip him to shreds and eat the remains.

Wally shook the feeling off. He couldn't let his rattled nerves get the better of him. For Leigh's sake, he must keep a clear head. He went another half a block, and stopped dead. An overturned car blocked the intersection. Debris was strewn everywhere. He started to go around and almost tripped over what he took to be part of a fender.

It was a body. To be exact, it was half a body, from the waist up, in a dried pool of blood. The head was turned to one side and bone gleamed where the cheek should be. The chin, too, had been gnawed clean. The eye was an empty socket.

Wally fought another impulse to heave. Fortunately, there wasn't anything left in his stomach to bring up. A few racking spasms, and he was over it and moved on.

The dead were everywhere. Or rather parts of them. Ravaged heads. Torn torsos. Limbs that had been ripped off. So many, it led Wally to surmise that a swarm of Kaiju Spawn had swept through town slaying everyone they came across.

Wally looked up from the litter of dead and spied another blockade ahead. Or so he assumed. He advanced slowly, praying he would find some soldiers still alive. But as he drew near, he was dumfounded to see that the blockade was a wall of people with their backs to him. He was about to call out when an icy bolt of fear rippled down his spine. They weren't people. They were Kaiju Spawn.

Wally froze. There could be no mistake. Scores of the things were just standing there, staring fixedly to the northeast. They swayed slightly, like reeds in the wind, and now and again one or another uttered a low hiss. He figured they must be resting. That they had sated their hunger on human flesh and had gone into some sort of somnolent state. Then he looked in the direction they were looking---and his very skin crawled.

Not quite a mile off, a gigantic form loomed against the backdrop of sparkling stars and the crescent moon. The Kaiju, itself, had stopped whether to rest or for some other purpose, Wally couldn't say. But there it stood, its massive bulk swaying slightly, just as the Kaiju Spawn were doing. Wally could swear that the swaying was synchronous, as if some sort of psychic link existed between the monster and the mutated aberrations it had spawned.

He had to get out of there while the Kaiju Spawn were distracted. Scarcely breathing, he crept to the curb and sought safety behind a hedge. To get a better idea of how many of the creatures blocked the road, he peered over, his heart leaping into his throat. They stretched for blocks. There must be hundreds.

Staying low, Wally moved from the hedge to a lilac bush and from there to the side of a house.

Once he was sure the Kaiju Spawn couldn't hear him, he broke into a run. He was only ten minutes or so from his old home, and from his daughter.

Other than a fence he had to clamber over, Wally made good time and soon came to the center of town. The main street was empty. No dead, no devastation. Probably, he reasoned, because the civil defense sirens had gone off and everyone had fled.

A lot of the buildings were brick, with awnings to shade pedestrians. He could see the white spire of a church, and the dome of the library. The electricity was out and everything was dark. Not so much as a candle flickered.

He had gone a couple of blocks when a low rumbling drew his attention to the Kaiju. The monster was moving again. The *thoom* of its first step was like a peal of thunder. With ponderous tread, it headed north, continuing on its mysterious way to who-knew-where. The cadence of the Kaiju's footfalls was like the beat of a bass drum, and as measured as a metronome.

Smiling, Wally let out a sigh of relief. At least the behemoth had spared Sylva. The same couldn't be said of the Kaiju Spawn, though, as became apparent when loud snarls and hisses erupted behind him. Now that their leviathan lord and master was on the move, so were the Kaiju Spawn. And they were coming in his direction.

Wally ran. The slap of his feet sounded unnaturally loud. He passed small shops and a hair salon and was almost to a restaurant when his footfalls were echoed by a flurry to his rear. Glancing over his shoulder, he distinguished shapes loping incredibly fast, with a strange lopsided gait. The swiftest of the pack. He doubted---he prayed---they hadn't seen him, but they would at any moment.

The restaurant door was open. Wally plunged inside, quietly shut the door, and backpedaled until he bumped against a chair. Grabbing it before it could topple to the floor; he ran to the counter and ducked behind it. The P-90 clutched to his chest, he struggled to control his breathing.

Putting an eye to the edge, Wally braced for the worst. Several Kaiju Spawn ran past, their bodies hunched forward, like bloodhounds on the scent. One was actually sniffing the air. They went by without looking at the restaurant, which told him they didn't know he was there. Luck was with him, yet his frustration was boundless. To be so close to his daughter, and have this happen.

Wally was about to go in search of a back door when a creature came to a stop right outside. It was sniffing, like the others, and turned its reptilian head from side to side. Suddenly it stepped to the window and peered in, its eyes seeming to glow with reflected moonlight.

"Please, no," Wally whispered.

The Kaiju Spawn stepped back and cocked a fist as if to smash the plate glass. Its gaze alighted on the door. Going over, it gripped the knob and shook it. When the door failed to open, it threw back its scaly head and gave voice to an eerie howl. Wrenching harder, it threw its shoulder against the frame. The door opened so suddenly that the Kaiju Spawn stumbled, and then recovered its balance. Hissing, it surveyed the interior.

Wally backed away from the counter. If he cut loose with the P-90, the shots might bring others. A narrow hall offered the possibility of escape. It was dark as sin. Backpedaling, he went about halfway, and halted.

The Kaiju Spawn was at the counter, its nose high, turning its head back and forth. Venting a loud hiss, it vaulted over, landed on all fours, and like a greyhound released on a race track, shot into the hallway after him.

Wally had no choice. He leveled the P-90, flicked the selector to full auto, and fired. It was a shot he couldn't possibly miss at such close range. A hail of lead struck the creature and jolted it to a stop. . . But only momentarily. The P-90's magazine held fifty rounds, enough to turn anyone, or anything, into Swiss cheese. Yet somehow the creature kept coming. It was almost to him, an out-flung claw inches from his face, when it collapsed. Gurgling and thrashing, it made a last furious effort to reach him, and was still.

"Damn," Wally gasped. Ejecting the spent magazine, he inserted another.

The back door, thankfully, wasn't locked. He eased out and gratefully gulped the fresh night air. The smart thing was to go slow but he was anxious for Leigh. With so many Kaiju Spawn about, if she was still alive, she was in dire danger. '*If*'. The most terrible of words, especially to a parent.

Tapping into a reservoir of energy he didn't know he possessed, Wally jogged half a dozen blocks and came to another residential section. Home---rather, his former home---was just up the street. Memories washed over him, of the happy times when his wife still loved him and the two of them doted over their precious little girl. The mere thought of her being torn to pieces....

Wally came within sight of their house. Overcome with emotion, he stopped and murmured Leigh's name. Hissing in the distance brought him out of himself. Now wasn't the time to be sentimental.

Despite an urge to dash straight to the front door, Wally circled the house. All appeared peaceful. Yet he couldn't shake a feeling that something was wrong. He was almost to the side door that opened onto the flower garden his wife was so fond of when he spotted a body. Human, not Kaiju Spawn, belly down. He nudged it with a toe, then rolled it over. "Howard!" he blurted.

Claudia's boyfriend had met a grisly end. His throat had been torn out, his gut ripped open.

Strands of his intestines lay stretched out around his body like purple, bloated snakes.

Wally felt no remorse. How could he? He had never liked the guy. Truth was, he'd wanted to bash his face in for coming between him and his wife. Clearly Howard had fallen prey to a Kaiju Spawn. But if so, where were Claudia…and Leigh?

Any caution evaporated in his concern for his daughter. Throwing the side door open, Wally entered. There was no light but he didn't need any. He knew this house like he knew the back of his hand. Leigh's bedroom was upstairs, the second room on the left. He took the stairs three at a stride and was going to call her name but the cry died in his throat as he turned to stone with his foot raised.

Claudia was at the top of the stairs, waiting for him. Or what had once been Claudia. Her tongue flicked out, rimming teeth as sharps as nails, and she grinned as if she were happy to see him. Almost as if she had been waiting for him. Lying in ambush for this very moment.

Surely not, Wally thought. And then his ex-wife shrieked and sprang, and damn if it didn't sound as if she shrieked his name. He fired a heartbeat before she slammed into him. Locked together, they fell. Her fetid breath fanned his neck as her teeth snapped an inch from his skin. They struck and bounced and tumbled, and Wally came to rest at the bottom, the wind knocked out of him, with her on top.

Claudia grinned that ghastly grin. She had him where she wanted him. Spreading her teeth, she bent. And who was to say which of them was the more surprised when Wally, without thinking, jammed the muzzle of the P-90 into her mouth and squeezed the trigger. Her head burst, showering gore and blood and hair on the wall and the floor. She fell across him, her once lovely eyes, now snake-like, fixed on his in hatred where once there had been love. Frantically, he shoved her off and rose, shaking.

A conflicting tide of emotions washed over him but Wally refused to give in to them. He could only think of Leigh. Flying up the stairs, he reached her door and hesitated. What if his wife had gotten to her? What if Leigh had suffered the same fate as Howard? Girding himself, he said softly, "Leigh? It's daddy. Are you in there?"

Wally opened the door.

****

Leigh's room was just as he remembered it. There were posters of Wonder Woman and Pinky Pie covering the walls. Stacks of comics lay scattered about the room's floor. His old Rom the Space Knight figure he had given her sat on Leigh's desk, well cared for, and looking every inch the valiant guardian and protector of humanity that the character had been in his comic series. There was no sign of Leigh though.

"Leigh," Wally called again, praying to hear an answer. None came.

Wally could hear a pack of Kaiju Spawn shuffling along the street outside. They had to have heard the gunfire from his encounter with Claudia. Wally moved to the room's sole window and risked a glance outside.

Three of the Kaiju Spawn were standing in the middle of the road outside the house. The creatures were sniffing the air, their heads twisting on their necks, craning around from one house on the street to another as if in search of where the noise they had heard came from.

Wally carefully crept back away from the window inwardly saying a prayer of thanks that the creatures didn't seem to know where he was. He stood in the shadows of his daughter's bedroom, listening, waiting to see what the Kaiju Spawn would do.

After a long moment, the creatures seemed to move on, the sound of their grunts and hisses fading into the distance. Only then did Wally move.

Moving as silently as he could, he headed downstairs. Claudia's nearly headless body twitched as he stepped over it. Wally nearly let loose on her corpse again with a fully automatic spray of bullets but caught his trigger finger at the last moment. Scared as he was he knew Claudia was dead and that doing so would only call the Kaiju Spawn that may still be outside to him.

Wally paused at the bottom of the stairs. Where in the devil was Leigh? She had to be here somewhere. The odds that she would venture outside were next to nothing given the circumstances. No, Leigh was a smart kid. She would find somewhere to hide and wait for help to come.

"The basement," Wally muttered, cursing himself for not thinking of it earlier. Throughout her childhood, they had always taken shelter there when there was trouble. He remembered the big storm that had rolled through when she was seven. They had holed up there for an entire day waiting for it to pass, playing board games by flashlight and listening to a battery powered radio.

The entrance to the basement was in the rear of the house's kitchen area. It took every ounce of his willpower not to run to the kitchen at a full out sprint. He crept through the living room, keeping his back to the wall and as far from its large windows as the space of the furniture-cramped room allowed him.

He eased around the corner doorway into the kitchen and froze. The place looked like a war zone. The table was overturned and splintered into pieces that littered the floor in front of him. The refrigerator hung open, swaying slowly back and forth on a single, still attached hinge. The small window above the sink was shattered and shards of broken glass glinted in the weak rays of moonlight that leaked in from the sky outside.

Relief washed over him as he saw the basement door was closed. The wood of its thick surface was covered in the claw marks of Kaiju Spawn and the wall around it showed clear signs of being attacked.

Wally rushed to the door, trying it, to find it locked. He heaved his shoulder into it and grunted in pain realizing that if one or more Kaiju Spawn couldn't smash through it easily, he sure wasn't going to be able to.

Wally leaned up against the door, pressing the side of his face into it. "Leigh," he called desperately. "Leigh, it's me. It's dad. If you're can hear me, please open the door."

Something moved in the basement. He could hear whatever it was underneath him. He held his breath as he listened to the sound of someone or something climbing the stairs to the other side of the door.

"Dad?" Leigh's voice answered him. "Is that really you?"

Wally started to respond to her but the words caught in his throat. Tears well up in his eyes and burst out to slide down over his cheeks. He nodded his head, knowing she couldn't see him, as he knees nearly gave out.

"Dad?" Leigh's voice called again.

"I'm. . .I'm here Leigh," he croaked.

He waited for the sounds of things being shifted about on the other side of the door, his heart pounding in his chest. When Leigh opened the door, he swept her up into his arms, letting his P-90 clatter to the kitchen floor. He hugged her so tightly that she slapped his shoulders and squealed.

"Easy dad!"

Sitting her down, he took a step back, drinking in the sight of her. She was even more beautiful than he remembered. Leigh's long blonde hair was dirty and unwashed. Her cheeks were stained with dirt and dust from the basement below. The T shirt she wore was tattered and her jeans blackened in patches by what appeared to be dried blood.

She flung herself back into his arms, sobbing.

"Mom. . ." she started but Wally cut her off.

"She's gone Leigh. She can't hurt you now."

"The bad things killed Howard," Leigh told him.

"I know," Wally said. "You were really smart to hide in the basement Leigh."

"It was all like a nightmare, Dad. The TV started

talking about those monsters. Mom and Howard didn't believe any of what the news was saying at first, but then we all saw a group of big army helicopters fly over the house. There was this awful noise way off in the distance, sort of like thunder but it wasn't. It was more like a roar. Mom and Howard started to believe what the TV had said. They started acting scared. I mean really scared. They were trying not to show it but I could tell. Howard got his shotgun out of the closet upstairs and loaded it as we all sat in the living room together. The TV had stopped talking by then. Every channel was just snow and static. It was like Mom and Howard didn't know what to do. Mom wanted us all to go to the basement and lock the door. Howard wanted us to get in the car and leave town. They argued . . . a lot."

Wally held onto Leigh as she told her story, his heart breaking for her. No kid should ever have to live through something like what the world was becoming. It just wasn't fair.

"Howard wouldn't stop demanding that we leave. Mom caved in. They sent me upstairs to get a few of my things while Howard went out to make sure it was safe and get the car ready to go. Howard never came back. Instead this thing came into the house. It was like a person but not. There were gray scales covering it and its eyes were yellow. I nearly peed myself when it burst through the front door. Wait. Dad, why do you smell like pee?"

Wally couldn't help but laugh. "I did pee myself on the road here honey, when I ran into one the monsters. I guess, in that sense, you were braver than I was."

Leigh giggled and Wally lit up inside. It was good to see that she was holding up well enough to still laugh.

"You were saying," Wally reminded her.

"Oh yeah," Leigh said and continued on with her tale. "The monster was covered in some sort of slime stuff too. Mom got between me and it. She fought it with a knife from the kitchen. Mom stuck the knife in the thing's throat and killed it. She told me to keep away from it and managed to drag its body out into the backyard. When she came back inside, she was sick. She just didn't look right ya know?"

"I understand," Wally nodded.

"Anyway, she told me not to touch her and told me to go on into the basement and lock the door and not to open it for anyone no matter what. I could hear Mom up here moving about. I wanted her to come down with me. After a while, it got quiet. I mean really quiet. I couldn't hear Mom anymore or anything else so I came up to check on her, only she wasn't in the kitchen."

Leigh's voice began to tremble and Wally knew what was coming next.

"Then I found her, only she wasn't Mom anymore. She had changed into one of those things. Her eyes were yellow just like the one she had killed. She. . .She came after me."

"And you ran," Wally stated.

Leigh nodded. "I ran back to the basement and got the door closed before she could get in. I've been there ever since. We had already stocked the basement with food, drinks, and a bunch of stuff. It wasn't so bad except for. . ."

"You did great Leigh," Wally beamed, trying to take her mind away from her memories. He knew that she had to have heard Claudia attacking the door. "You really did."

"Dad?" Leigh asked, staring up at him. "What do we do now? Are we leaving?"

Wally had no answer. He hadn't thought that far ahead. All his energy and focus had been on just finding Leigh. Now that he had, he had no idea what they were going to do.

They could go into the basement together and wait for help or they could try to make a run for it through the packs of Kaiju Spawn that stalked the streets of the town. Neither option was without risk.

"Do you want to leave?" Wally asked.

Leigh nodded.

"Okay then," Wally said, releasing her. "To do that, we are going to need a plan."

****

Howard's car was still parked in the driveway in front of the house. Wally knew he wouldn't have time to hotwire it if they used it. The Kaiju Spawn would be on them fast as soon as they left the house. Thankfully, Leigh knew where Claudia and Howard kept a spare set of keys for it. Wally set Leigh to gathering up some supplies for them, to keep her busy and out of trouble, while he tried to figure out the best means by which to get to the car. If they could make it to the parked vehicle, they would still be far from out of the woods but at least they would have a chance.

Wally couldn't come up with anything better than just rushing the car though and hoping the Kaiju Spawn were a good distance away when they did.

When Leigh returned from the kitchen to join him in the corner of the living room, he sat her down.

"This is going to be dangerous Leigh," he warned her. "We're going to have to move fast and you're going to have to do exactly what I say out there without any backtalk. Do you understand?"

Leigh nodded. "I got it Dad."

And Wally believed that she did.

"Let's give it a few more minutes just to make sure there are none of those things out there waiting for us in the bushes and then we'll go when I say."

There was really no reason to wait in terms of what they were about to try. If the Kaiju Spawn were waiting on them, the things were doing a bang up job of keeping quiet which wasn't something

Wally imagined was well inside their wheelhouse. In truth, Wally just wanted to spend a few more peaceful, well, as peaceful as a Kaiju filled world allowed, moments with his little girl.

"It's all going to be okay Leigh," he lied.

Leigh reached out and took his hand in hers. "I know it will be Dad . . .because you're here."

Wally squeezed her hand tight then let go.

"You ready?" he asked.

Leigh nodded.

"Stay with me now," he cautioned, moving to the front door and opening it. He took a last look at his little girl over his shoulder then shouted, "Go!"

Wally dived through the doorway, Leigh hot on his heels. He sprinted down the drive towards Howard's car.   Up the street, Wally saw one of the Kaiju Spawn. It saw him too, its yellow eyes locking onto him, filled with vile depths of hatred and hunger. The Kaiju Spawn laid back its head and unleashed a roar that tore the night.

Wally paused, knowing he shouldn't, and lifted the P-90 to his shoulder. He took aim and put a round through the Kaiju Spawn's head. It dropped where it stood, its body twitching on the ground as its brains leaked from its ruptured skull.

Leigh darted by Wally and got into the car, slamming and locking the passenger side door after her. Wally allowed himself a smile, proud she had done as he had told her to do instead of stopping at his side.

Between the Kaiju Spawn's roar and the gunshot, any chance of getting out of the drive before they were spotted was gone. More of the Kaiju Spawn came. They appeared at both ends of the block and bounded towards the house's drive as Wally slid into the driver seat of the car. Others were pouring out of the houses that lined the street as Wally shoved the keys into the car's ignition and cranked the engine.

"Dad!" Leigh screamed, gesturing at the house behind them. There were Kaiju Spawn there too. They came running around the sides of the house, howling and raging as they closed in on the car.

Wally jerked the car into reverse and put his foot down on the gas. The car shot out of the drive backwards. He whipped the wheel around, turning the car northward towards the smaller of the two large packs of Kaiju and floored the gas this time.

The Kaiju Spawn made no attempt to get out of the car's path. It was like a sick game of chicken that Wally knew he couldn't afford to lose.

The car plowed into the ranks of the Kaiju Spawn, flinging some aside while others were knocked from their feet and dragged under the wheels of the car. Wally fought with all his might to keep the car under control. It wasn't built for the Hell it was enduring and he could only pray it kept running long enough to get them through.

The impacts of the Kaiju slowed the car but it did keep going. Kaiju Spawn came at it from the sides before it began to pick up speed again. Their claws scraped at its sides, raking away paint and causing sparks to fly in the semi-darkness of the moonlit night. The window next to Leigh caved inward, showering her with broken glass. Leigh was screaming at the top of her lungs as Wally barked, "Get down!"

Leigh ducked in her seat as Wally fired the P-90 over her. He let the Kaiju Spawn trying to hold onto the side of the car and claw its way inside have it. A stream of automatic rounds ripped the creature's face to shreds before its limp body released the side of the car and it went rolling along the road in the car's wake.

"Stay down!" Wally ordered as he refocused his attention on the road in front of the car. They had made it through the primary pack of Kaiju Spawn though more of the creatures were pouring into the road from its sides and trying to get into the vehicle's path to intercept it.

Wally took the bend at the end of the block hard. The car bounced over the curb but kept moving.

Then Leigh sat up in her seat, took a quick glance around, and yelled, "We made it Dad!"

And she was right. They were on the main road out of town now and the only Kaiju Spawn to be seen were shrinking dots in the rearview mirror.

"We did, didn't we?" Wally laughed, long and loud.

"Dang right we did!" Leigh shouted.

They drove on without saying another word for several minutes after they hit the interstate proper. Wally knew what had just happened was nothing short of an honest to goodness miracle.

"Try the radio," Wally said breaking the silence.

Leigh clicked it on and ran the gamut of stations.

There was nothing on the air.

Wally noticed Leigh frowning.

"Don't worry kiddo," he told her. "We got this."

She didn't look as if she believed him.

"We made it out of there didn't we?" He asked with a smile. "Trust me kiddo, we're gonna be just fine."

Wally thumped a palm against the steering wheel as he drove, acting excited. "The whole world is out there waiting on us, so tell me Leigh, where do you want to go?"

"You pick Dad," She said, her frown vanishing as quickly as it had appeared. "As long as I'm with you, I know it's going to be okay too."

Wally's smile stretched his lips to their limits. "Okay," he gestured towards the rising sun, "Straight on to the horizon kiddo. Straight on together."

Somewhere behind them the giant Kaiju gave a roar that shook the ground underneath the moving car but they both ignored it, keeping their eyes on the road ahead.

END

David Robbins is the author of over three hundred published novels including the internationally famous *ENDWORLD* series and the new *ANGEL U* series. Some of his other works include The *WILDERNESS* series and the novelizations of the films *PROOF OF LIFE* (Staring Russell Crowe) and *MEN OF HONOR* (Staring Robert De Niro). His books have been translated into nine languages and sold millions of copies worldwide. He is a member of the Horror Writers Association, the Science Fiction and Fantasy Writers of America, and the Western Writers of America.

Eric S Brown is the author of numerous series including the Bigfoot War series, The Kaiju Apocalypse series (with Jason Cordova), and the Crypto-Squad series with Jason Brannon. Some of his stand alone works include Megalodon, Night of the Kaiju, Dawn of the Kaiju, World War of the Dead, Sasquatch Lake, and War of the Worlds Plus Blood Guts and Zombies. His short fiction has been published hundreds of times in the small press and beyond including in markets such the Onward Drake anthology from Baen Books, the Grantville Gazette, and Walmart World Magazine. Two of his books have been made into feature films- Bigfoot War (2014) from Origin Releasing and Werewolf Massacre at Hell's Gate (2015) from Ingy Films. He lives in North Carolina with his wife and two children where he continues to write tales of giant monsters, blazing guns, hungry corpses, and the things that lurk in the woods.

www.ingramcontent.com/pod-product-compliance
Lightning Source LLC
Chambersburg PA
CBHW060955120626
46557CB00003B/1178